THE GREAT DRAKE

THE
GREAT

Illustrations by Fred Charle.

1817

Published in San Francisco by

DRAKE

MARIO CAPPELLI

HARPER & ROW, PUBLISHERS

New York, Hagerstown, San Francisco, London

*A story especially for Anthony, who still
knows that birds and animals can laugh,
feel joy and sorrow... and do great things.*

FIRST EDITION

Designed by Jim Mennick

ISBN: 0-06-061303-3

LIBRARY OF CONGRESS CATALOG CARD NUMBER: 77-7840

77 78 79 80 81 82 10 9 8 7 6 5 4 3 2 1

THE WINTER of 1886–87 swept down from the Arctic on a rage of winds, bringing heavy snows and subzero temperatures that would continue relentlessly for more than one hundred days. Bitter winds froze man and beast in their tracks, their bodies not to be found until spring. Snow piled up on the frozen ground and drifted to monumental heights, burying the structures built by man and trapping his livestock far from food and shelter. Wolves, maddened with hunger, came down from the mountains and fought the coyote for the weak, the dead, and the dying. Thousands of waterfowl that had summered in the Arctic were lost; blinded and confused by the driving snow, they crashed to the ground, never to arise.

THE snow geese were the first to assemble. Having moved from the marshes and waters of the coastal shores to the southwest, they settled on these inland lakes for rest, feeding, and gossip and to await the arrival of the other species of waterfowl that would share with them the long flight north. Soon they were joined by the whistling swans, followed shortly by the trumpeter swans. And every day flocks of ducks appeared.

Noisily, as their numbers swelled, the flocks continued the business of feeding themselves for the long journey. Poking, rummaging, and diving for any morsel nature would provide, they filled themselves to capacity and then began all over again. Those who had been there for a week or more were anxious to be off. But departure was uncertain. There were storms to the north—storms that could block migration for many days. They would have to wait for the Great Drake. He would lead them around the storms; he would guide them safely to their summer lands.

The weeks became a month, and March gave way to April. Now the gathering of flocks was larger than any could remember. Arguments broke out over the choicest feeding and resting places. The younger ones amused themselves in reckless play; they chased each other across the waters, ignoring the warnings of their elders to beware the hungry predators that stalked the banks.

The concerned and the frightened reported to the leaders of the flocks. "Some have already fallen victim to the deadly jaws of the fox and the sharp talons of the hawk. More will be lost each day. The flocks grow restless. Soon we must leave."

"Rest and feed," the leaders advised. "Soon the Great Drake will come and we shall move as one."

"He must come soon," a fearful one whispered to his neighbor, "or all our young will surely be devoured." And the neighbor whispered it to his neighbor who whispered it to another and yet another until the entire gathering was aroused and ready to depart at once.

"Where is he?" they demanded. "Why isn't he

here? For days we have been waiting for the Great Drake—a Great Drake no one has ever seen."

"The Great Drake will come," the leaders promised. "Calm yourselves. Rest and feed for the long journey." But as the days passed and there was still no sign of the Great Drake, questions became more frequent and filled with anger.

"Where is he?"

"Who needs him?"

"How do we know he will come?"

"Let's go without him."

"No," said the elders, "we must be patient. Terrible storms have been reported all along the northern route. Swirling winds. Winds that topple everything in their path. Some have sucked the very soil of the land into their gaping funnels and blown it out the tops of towering clouds. Lakes have been turned into raging seas, and ponds and rivers have been lifted from their beds and dropped many miles away. Already many have perished. We must wait for the Great Drake. He will know when it is safe to fly north. To proceed by individual flock without him would be foolish, risky, and ultimately disastrous."

But the gathering was not convinced. "There have been terrible storms, we know," they argued, "but they do not rage unbroken. It would be a simple matter to approach the storm area, land and wait for the skies to clear, and then take off. All the flocks would be well north before another line of storms could form behind them, no matter how terrible they might be."

"If our leaders will not guide us, I will!" a voice cried out. And soon a hundred or more voices joined in, each promising to lead the flocks. Arguments became animated and the words insulting and threatening until they stirred the very passions of the resting flocks. Soon all were shouting in support of their chosen champions, and fights became frequent and vicious.

Suddenly a large bird descended into the midst of this turmoil and crying high above the noise, challenged all to test their strength against his, rather than fight meaninglessly among themselves. One by one he took on those who agreed to fight him, and one by one he bested them, without doing them serious injury. Soon no more would test him.

"Who is this challenger?" they asked each other. "Has he come to lead us?"

"I am as you," said the Challenger, "recently up from the south. I have not come to lead, but to see the Great Drake."

"If you best him will you lead us?" asked one he had just defeated.

"No one may challenge the Great Drake! And only the Great Drake may lead you! None may replace him!" he replied sharply. "That is, if he exists. I have never seen him. My parents had never seen him, yet they, like all the fowl of the air, whispered his name.

But I shall see for myself. No longer shall I listen to
whispers."

"It has been told," said one of the elders, "that the Great Drake is a title given to the leader of all the flocks regardless of his size or species; that he may even be of a type we do not now recognize. Do you believe this to be true?"

"It is possible," the Challenger said, nodding slowly, "though it is also told that the first Great Drake was indeed a mallard of unusual size and strength."

"It is also said that the Great Drake is older than any now alive. Could this be so?"

"Perhaps," replied the Challenger. "Certainly a Great Drake has not been proclaimed during my lifetime or in the time of my parents. So, if a Great Drake lives, he was elevated by the flocks before the birth of any now alive."

"What then of a Noble One and a Very Noble One? Such titles may only be given by the Great Drake, and it is said that none now hold these titles."

"This, too, I think to be true," the Challenger answered. "I have not heard of any Noble Ones yet living."

"Then it is reasonable to assume that a Great Drake does not now live. If it were otherwise he certainly would have elevated at least one to the position of Noble One."

"To this I cannot reply. Yet many of our elders and

leaders believe that a Great Drake lives and that he will appear to lead all the flocks."

With these words the Challenger moved away from the center of the throng, leaving them to their noisy discussions. He had stopped the fighting; more he could not do. And he had to admit, such intensive combat, exhilarating as it was, had tired him, and he needed rest.

But he was not to rest for long. In less than an hour a clamor of voices demanded his attention.

"We are agreed!"

"We believe that no Great Drake now lives!"

"And we wish to elevate you to Great Drake!"

The words and the offer so stunned the Challenger, he leaped into the air and climbed rapidly to a thousand feet.

"I have been victorious over your most powerful fighters," he proclaimed loudly so that he could be heard over the cheering below. "I have flown faster than your most swift. But a Great Drake I shall never be. Such an honor is out of the question. I do not seek it! I do not want it! And you may not offer it!"

"Then we shall seek another who *will* accept!" they countered, and began chattering among themselves.

"Seek, then!" he called down to them. "But a Great Drake you will not find among us. Such a leader would be known to all by his very presence."

Alone in the sky, he was troubled. He had fought

fairly and proved himself the strongest, yet he felt less than he was before. None would want to face him again in friendly combat, and now his sharp words of rejection had offended many and set him further apart from the flocks. For the first time in his life he experienced loneliness.

His thoughts were interrupted by an ever-growing chatter from the ground. At first he had difficulty understanding what they were saying and the reason for their excitement. Then it became quite clear as word was passed from flock to flock.

"He's coming!"

"He's been sighted to the northwest!"

"He comes! He will be here soon!" Their excitement became an uncontrollable roar, and by the thousands they rose as high as their legs and necks would permit and beat their wings joyously on the waters.

"The Great Drake comes!" they chanted, while those in the air flew in strange erratic patterns, falling, tumbling, flipping over, and then racing to see who would be the first to land that he might enjoy the best vantage point. They all seemed to be asking questions at once. "Is he big . . . powerful . . . swift . . . faster than the flashing light that runs from black clouds?"

Most admitted that they did not know, for they had never seen him, while others, who had not seen him either, puffed up their feathers and craned their necks with importance.

"He is all of those things and more," one boasted.

"He's over a hundred years old," said his neighbor, bobbing his small head with assurance.

"He can't be that old," another argued. "No one is that old."

"Well, he's fifty, at least," said a large gander, working his way through the group until he reached the center.

"How do you know?" he was asked by many voices.

"Because I've seen him!" he announced, pausing to preen his feathers and listen to the gasps that came from every mouth. Everyone drew closer, tightening the circle, as word was passed that here was someone who had actually seen the Great Drake.

The center of attraction was indeed a large bird, appearing every inch the size and stature of the Challenger as he puffed and strutted in their midst.

"He was a long way off, to be sure," he continued, as all strained to hear his words. Groans of disappointment came from those nearest him, but the Center of Attraction quickly dispelled any doubts. "However, I have excellent eyesight, and I saw him quite clearly." His patrician manner and the way he fluffed his black-tipped glossy white feathers captivated them.

"He *saw* him! He saw the Great Drake as if he were flying alongside him," someone shouted in response. Quickly word was flashed back, rank upon rank, that the Center of Attraction had not only seen the Great

Drake, but knew him personally, swam with him, and even called him friend.

"It is rumored," said one in the rear ranks, "that the Center of Attraction will be elevated to a Noble One or perhaps even a Very Noble One when the Great Drake arrives."

"He should be," his neighbor agreed, "inasmuch as he has been an advisor to the Great Drake for many years."

"His wingspan is truly enormous!" the Center of Attraction continued in a loud voice, and then paused so that all might visualize the monumental reach of the Great Drake's spread.

This new information spread rapidly. "He has enormous wings! Truly monumental! Indeed, when the Great Drake flies through the rain, the ground beneath remains dry for a considerable period afterward! Then when he is ready to land he simply shakes his feathers and a lake forms for his use and rest."

The Challenger, hovering overhead, had heard enough, and bellowed out a long "aaaawaaakk!" His cry of skepticism, however, was ignored by those on the ground, for they were enchanted by the words and promises of the Center of Attraction.

Now the flock leaders and elders assembled about the Center of Attraction, and he addressed them personally. "I will certainly advise him to lead us north with the morning sun," he said. "Of course, he is the

Great Drake and the final decision is up to him, but when I offer my advice and counsel I am certain he will be off with the first rays of dawn." The word flew back and the flocks were advised to prepare for their long journey with the first light, or perhaps even sooner.

The Challenger climbed high above the earth, laughing in spite of himself, and headed northwest. It's a wonder the Center of Attraction didn't tell everyone that *he* is the Great Drake, he thought. Certainly thousands would believe him and readily follow.

The sun had been hidden behind some clouds most of the afternoon; now it emerged suddenly, and the Challenger flew directly into its blinding glare. Just as he decided to change his course, he saw something that nearly froze him motionless. Coming toward him right out of the sun was a fantastic creature with wings that extended beyond its glowing rim.

It can't be! he told himself. Nothing can be that large—and fly. Perhaps the Center of Attraction had been telling the truth after all.

Carefully, he tilted his head to avoid looking directly into the sun, and began studying the massive creature. To his amazement, it began to break up into a formation of three.

He rose fifty feet for a better view, and after banking into a series of shallow turns, waited for the formation to pass under him. Then he began to descend. Soon he could make out every feather of two large snow

geese and the largest, most magnificent white swan he
had ever seen. She was a creature of inexpressible grace
and beauty. Her enormous wings—and they were truly
enormous—seemed to caress the air in a rhythm of
majestic harmony. He was totally captivated by her
and felt himself being drawn closer as if by some irre-
sistible force. Although he was by no means a small
bird, she was more than twice his size and could easily
have destroyed him with a single swipe of her wing.
Still, she did not waver in her flight; nor did she so
much as tilt her head to look at him.

"Who are you and what is your purpose?"

The words caught him completely by surprise. He
had been so fascinated by the sweeping thrusts of the
white swan's great wings that he had failed to see one
of the snow geese drop back and fall into formation
with him. Although the question had not been voiced
as a threat, it was couched in authority, and he hastened to reply.

"I am known as the Challenger," he said, "because
I enjoy the sport of friendly combat. As for my purpose, I have come to greet the Great Drake. But I do
not see him here—unless you are the Great Drake and
I have been mistaken."

"Greetings, Challenger," the snow goose said. "But
it is not I you seek."

"Your companion, then?"

"No," the snow goose replied, and began speeding

up to close the gap between them and the white swan, who had moved some distance ahead. Soon they were directly above her and again the Challenger knew her to be the most beautiful and graceful swan he had ever seen or dreamed existed. He was completely enraptured by her power and poetry of motion.

The white swan, however, still maintained a singular indifference to his presence. Then suddenly she began to drop back. Almost directly beneath her, certainly not more than twenty feet below her sweeping wing tips, there was something . . . something that remotely resembled a swan, but ever so remotely. The long neck was there, and the general contours, but that was all.

While the white swan moved her wings in perfect rhythm, the bird over whom she flew like some protective curtain moved his awkwardly and with obvious difficulty, one faster than the other. In fact, it was clearly evident that his right wing was shorter than his left and that an entire grouping of feathers that should have formed its tip was missing.

"Such a thing can't fly!" the Challenger cried out loud. But if the thing heard, he ignored the Challenger's presence, and continued the labored, uneven beat of his wings.

As the Challenger closed to within a few yards of the strange bird he noted further that his tail fan contained no more than a half-dozen, nearly bare quills that concealed little of the coarse and wrinkled flesh beneath. Certainly, they would be unequal to the task of balancing and braking during the last moments of the landing run.

Every landing must be a personal disaster, the Challenger thought. He must damage something every time he drops down.

They were beginning to descend, and the Challenger followed closely behind. He has not glanced my way, let alone acknowledged my existence, he thought, and yet I want to follow him. I must follow him. He is the Great Drake! I know this to be true.

The two snow geese suddenly increased their rate of descent, leaving the others behind. Moving in low over the lake they had selected for a landing site, they turned into the wind and settled upon the water with hardly a ripple. Those members of the flocks gathered in the area backed away. But from his position several hundred feet above, the Challenger could see that their necks were stretched to their limits, and their heads were pointed toward the three preparing to land. Their eyes were wide with disbelief. The Challenger they recognized, of course, and a great white swan— but what of the third? Truly, it was like nothing they had seen before, and for the moment they were struck dumb.

The Challenger began a series of shallow circles. He did not want to interfere with the Great Drake's landing approach or get in the way of the white swan. The approach was fast—too fast. There could be no question that the Great Drake's shortened wing and lack of tail feathers presented him with a handicap of considerable proportions. Lower and lower he dropped, his right wing noticeably out of phase with his left, causing control problems of increasing magnitude. His body continually rolled to the right, and he was experiencing major difficulties in just maintaining level flight. To correct for the roll he dropped his legs; and for the first time the Challenger saw that half of the right foot was missing. The Challenger shook his head in amazement while those below gasped in horror. The right leg, too, was slightly bent out of shape, possibly having been broken when the foot was half shorn away. Now the Great Drake turned his twisted limb so that the half-foot was presented edgewise to the air current, thus providing directional control as would a rudder.

But he was not yet safely on the water, and even with his foot acting as a rudder, he continued to roll dangerously to the right, especially during the final moments of the landing run. When it appeared that his right wing could no longer support him and that he would roll completely over, he quickly folded his wings and with the strength of his body alone snapped himself upright. Practice, determination, and a special need for survival provided the final degree of control that permitted him to descend to within three feet of the water. Then, retracting his feet, he tumbled in a

half-roll to the right, crashed to the surface, and sub-
merged. The snow geese had been careful to select the
proper depth of water, and in a moment, as though it
were a quiet, uneventful landing, he surfaced.

"What is *this* that arrives? A crippled fowl of unde-
termined and questionable species!" It was the Center
of Attraction who spoke, and many, listening to his
ridicule, made ugly sounds. "He is an impostor!" he
continued with a contemptuous hiss. "Certainly not
the Great Drake that I know!"

For a moment the Great Drake looked at them in
silence. Then he swam off to the bank of a quiet cove,
and looping his thin neck back so that his head rested
over his good wing, slept.

There was quiet over the lake and marshland, except
for a whisper that travelled from flock to flock.

"An impostor!"

W HO *is* he?"

The question was passed from flock to flock and none could answer. The Challenger meanwhile continued to circle, watching and listening with interest to the events unfolding on the lake below. It did not seem right that any would question the identity of the Great Drake. The one that had arrived could be no other. The very fact that he could fly at all with such severe handicaps should be evidence enough to convince the most doubting skeptic. Then there were the injuries themselves. How often had the Challenger heard stories of the remarkable feats of courage and daring performed by the Great Drake while leading the flocks or rescuing individual members. He had never tired of those stories, especially those in which the Great Drake saved entire flocks from annihilation while ignoring his own injuries—injuries so severe and incapacitating that they would have felled all others.

Still, he had to admit that the first sight of the Great Drake had not been what he had expected. Somehow, he had never visualized the Great Drake with lasting injuries. A Great Drake, he had thought in his youth, should be able to suffer the loss of a wing, a leg, or tail feathers and very soon sprout new ones. The Great Drake had seemed very real to him then. But by the time he had set out on his own, he regarded the stories as more fantasy than fact, and indeed, considered the Great Drake to be a legendary figure who lived in the minds of the very young and the very old.

The group of supporters that had gathered around the Center of Attraction were still making nasty sounds, aroused and inflamed by his angry denunciation.

"He is not the Great Drake!" the Center of Attraction cried angrily. "He is an impostor, a cripple seeking the honors and homage due another! He should be driven from this place and destroyed that he may never again assume that which he is not!"

Suddenly those gathered around the Center of Attraction turned toward the Great Drake. A few began to close in on him, their voices venomous and ugly.

The Challenger, still circling above, began a dive that would have placed him squarely in their midst, but stopped short when he saw the white swan unfold her enormous wings, stretch out her long slender neck, and face the advancing mob. She said not a word, but her attack posture conveyed the necessary warning: Move closer and you will terminate your days floating feet up in the water! The two snow geese also assumed an attack posture, presenting a defensive perimeter only the foolhardy would test.

Then, unaccountably, they relaxed and assumed a posture of simply watching and waiting. Considering the threat, this was a curious response. The Challenger was dumbfounded. Yet clearly the white swan and the snow geese were obeying the Great Drake. The Challenger immediately adjusted his flight pattern to remain in a position directly above the Center of Attraction, a position from which he could attack should this become necessary.

The mob had stopped when faced by the white swan and the snow geese. But now they moved in. This time the Challenger did not hesitate. He swooped down, nearly clipping the head of the Center of Attraction. The troublemakers scattered, paddling frantically for less hazardous water.

"I challenge the Center of Attraction to combat!" cried the Challenger. He thrust out his head and rattled his wings.

"Yes!" the cry went up from many voices. "The Center of Attraction must meet him in a fair show of strength."

"In the air or on the water, my friend?" asked the Challenger. "It's your choice."

"It shall be neither; your strength in combat I do not dispute," the Center of Attraction cried loudly so that all might hear, thus ending any further talk of combat. There were many groans of disappointment, now that the gathering was to be deprived of such a splendid spectacle.

"Your wisdom is not yet as well developed as your strength," the Center of Attraction hissed at the Challenger. His eyes were full of loathing and his voice quivered. "There will be another time, another place. Your strength will serve you little when next we meet."

"We shall never meet again," the Challenger said softly and without malice. He knew nothing of prophecy, and was surprised at his own words.

"We shall see!" The Center of Attraction arched his neck in scorn, then turned and flew away.

And there were those who followed him.

"Well done, Noble One."

The Challenger spun around to see who had spoken these words and to whom they were directed. He was facing the Great Drake.

"Well done, Noble One," the Great Drake repeated.

There were gasps of awe from the assembled flocks,
then excited whispers.

"This is truly the Great Drake! He is here in our
midst to lead us."

"And we have a Noble One!"

"The Challenger has been made a Noble One!"

"The Great Drake has proclaimed it!"

The newly named Noble One could not believe his
ears. He looked from the Great Drake to the cheering
flock and then back again. "I'm not worthy of . . ." he
began, hardly recognizing his own voice.

"You are indeed a Noble One," the Great Drake
said. "We are most pleased." He gave a nod of ap-
proval. The flocks cheered wildly.

"We have a Noble One!"

"The Great Drake has said it!"

"We have a Noble One!"

There was much rejoicing, for none had ever seen
a Great Drake, or a Noble One, and now the Challenger, whom they all knew, had just been given this
awesome title.

The Great Drake nodded again and then slowly
withdrew, the white swan and the snow geese closing
in about him. Soon he was resting peacefully again, his
long neck folded back over his wing.

Elevation to Noble One brought about an immediate change in the Challenger's way of life. Although he

was used to being treated with respect, he was not at all prepared for the homage he would now be paid. As he swam away from the Great Drake's resting place, the flocks backed away, opening a path for him.

"There is excellent feeding on the north bank," said one of the elders. "Wild rice, nourishing and tasty."

"Thank you. I am a little hungry, but I have no wish to take what you have found for yourselves. I shall hunt about myself and find ample feeding, I'm sure."

But they would not hear of it. Forming an escort, several of the leaders began moving toward the north bank and the Noble One followed, nodding to all who called to greet him.

"Welcome, Noble One. We are pleased to have you among us."

The Noble One approached the north bank, and it was as the elder had said; here was excellent feeding. He looked around, and found his escort at a respectful distance, and the flocks even further away. He felt a pang of loneliness. They are pleased to have a Noble One among them, he thought, but not as one of them.

He ate slowly and well. Yet he felt a heavy sadness, aware that but a few hours ago he could have joined any of the flocks, eaten with them, and enjoyed their stories. Now he was alone. I am a Noble One, he thought. This is an honor from which I cannot flee, though if the truth were known I would do so tonight.

THE days passed and still the Great Drake did not
ready the flocks. Twice the two snow geese were observed taking off and heading north. Each time they
were back by nightfall and quickly entered into discus-
sion with their leader. The Great Drake listened intently until they had completed their reports, and
thanked them. Then he swam off by himself, placed
his head back over his wing, and slept.

The flocks grew more restless by the hour. The Center of Attraction became active again. He preened his
feathers, and spoke to the flocks.

"I am ready to lead you," he declared, arching his
neck. "I have reason to believe that the Great Drake

can no longer fly. It has been reported that he suffered near-fatal injuries upon his landing, and many of us witnessed that frightful performance, didn't we?"

Those who had been hanging back uncertainly now nodded their heads in agreement. "It is true. Many of us were there and saw him crash into the water."

"He's dying, you know," others whispered.

Soon many thousands were convinced that the Great Drake could not lead them, and were ready to leave without him.

"We leave with the morning sun," announced the Center of Attraction.

A great cheer went up. "We'll follow you. The Great Drake is dying. Soon we shall have a new and more powerful Great Drake."

The Center of Attraction listened and was pleased.

By the next morning, all the flocks had learned of the Center of Attraction's plan to leave without the Great Drake. "We shall see about that!" the new Noble One promised himself when he heard the news. "I'll have to have a little talk with him." The sun was just beginning to warm the land when he set about searching for his adversary. After flying for about an hour he heard the summons from the flocks below.

"Greetings, Noble One. We are happy to have you among us. But please go to the resting place of the Great Drake, for word has been passed that he would be grateful for your presence."

The Noble One descended immediately. When he arrived at the quiet cove, the Great Drake was conversing with the two snow geese, who had just returned from one of their far-sweeping flights. They had been flying most of the night, and it was clear that they had encountered major problems, for they were tired and worn and in need of food and rest.

"Welcome, Noble One," said White Swan pleasantly, but even she backed away respectfully as he approached.

"Thank you, White Swan," he said, experiencing a warming sensation over his entire body and, at the same time, feeling ill at ease because of her homage. He wished he could talk with her just to hear her voice, for it was strangely comforting. But that would have to wait. The Great Drake summoned him to his side with a nod. The First Snow Goose was reporting on his mission.

"I proceeded north," he was saying. "The sky was clear for the first two hours. Then I encountered a thin layer of clouds that thickened rapidly and totally obscured the ground. Soon they dominated the sky, and I was forced to climb just to stay aloft. Struggling to remain above the clouds, I exceeded my flight limitations and fell several thousand feet before I was again capable of maintaining level flight."

"Did you actually enter the cloud tops?" the Great Drake asked.

"I fell through a layer that was not more than a few

hundred feet thick," the Snow Goose replied. "When I emerged I could see another much denser and darker layer far below me. But greater difficulties lay ahead. A few miles to the north the lower layer began to slant upward at a very steep angle and appeared to penetrate and rise above the layer through which I had fallen. When I began to climb again, I did so in shallow circles."

"Did you witness lightning in and about the lower layer, or feel any strong updrafts?"

"Much lightning was flashing across and through the entire lower layer, and the updrafts became stronger as I came closer to the slanting wall. Indeed, once I topped the upper layer, the updrafts drove me to even greater heights. I was forced to struggle for every yard of level flight. Slowly I maneuvered myself a few miles south, where I could descend to a lower altitude and consider my next course of action."

"You were most fortunate," the Great Drake said gravely.

"I was fortunate indeed. When I was once again in complete control I remained well south of that turbulent wall of clouds."

"And did you discover any openings to the west that might permit a flock of several thousand some assurance of safe passage?" the Great Drake asked.

"I did. Several hours' flight to the northwest the cloud tops appeared to drop significantly. And the wind, too, had altered in both strength and direction."

The news of the wind shift seemed to please the Great Drake, but when he turned to the Second Snow Goose his tone again became serious. "And what of the weather to the north and east?"

"High clouds. Twisting winds and heavy rains," the Second Snow Goose began. "From the very ground to the peaks of the sky the clouds controlled the air as far as the eye could see. It is true I found several small passages through which a small flock might have reached safety, but each was high in an otherwise solid wall of black, lightning-laced clouds. And the passages quickly closed as new clouds and fresh winds moved in."

"But could passage be made by a flock properly led?" the Great Drake asked anxiously.

"Such is possible," the Second Snow Goose replied with a slow nod, "but there are other dangers as well. As I was following the line of storm clouds that blocked all access north, still searching for an opening, I saw a strange series of white lines that seemed to emerge from one great cloud high above all the others. They etched a spidery pattern against the sky, a giant web without the supporting, interlacing strands. When they fell, they arched over like a spray of water. And . . ."

"Hail!"

"Yes, a massive outpouring of hail. I managed to fly

free, but not before taking several punishing blows to remind me of my foolishness."

"You, too, were most fortunate," said the Great Drake. "Such conditions as you describe are rare, especially for regions well to the north. But now, feed and rest. You have both done well. We are most pleased."

The Noble One, watching intently, noticed the glow of pleasure in the eyes of the Snow Geese at the Great Drake's praise.

"Thank you for your prompt response to my call," the Great Drake said, turning to the Noble One. "You have heard the reports?"

"Every word," the Noble One said. "The Snow Geese are to be commended for their comprehensive reports." He nodded to them as they were about to take their leave.

"We are pleased with the kind words of the Noble One," they said, nodding respectfully in return. Then they backed off to feed and rest.

"Such homage and formality make you feel ill at ease, I know," the Great Drake said when the Snow Geese were out of earshot. "But remember, respect for a Noble One is deeply ingrained in each individual— it is present even before birth—and you shall earn that respect every remaining day of your life. Even more deference is shown to a Very Noble One and to a Great Drake." There was a note of sorrow in his voice that spoke clearly of his own life. "You will learn to live with it and bear it with dignity."

"With your kind help."

"Come swim with me," the Great Drake invited. "I have something of greatest importance to tell you."

For some moments they glided along in silence, White Swan following a short distance behind, close enough to offer immediate protection, should that become necessary, but not close enough to intrude into the conversation.

"Early this morning," the Great Drake said, "an individual known to us as the Center of Attraction gathered a large flock under his leadership and is even now on his way north."

So he has already left, the Noble One thought, but said nothing.

"The flocks of course are free to follow any leader they wish." There were several minutes of silence, as the Great Drake seemed to study his reflection in the water. When he spoke again it was in slow, measured words. "I fear they face an ordeal for which they are not prepared . . ." His voice trailed off, and he fastened his gaze on a point far beyond the Noble One's vision. "Yes," he said, and now his words seemed meant more for himself than for the Noble One who strained to hear them. "The Center of Attraction is approaching a line of storms—a line he has already seen, but foolishly believes he can circumnavigate. He has seriously misjudged his own competence and the magnitude of the storms. Already they build behind him!"

The Noble One listened with growing astonishment. Could the Great Drake actually see things as they happened? How was this possible?

The Great Drake continued, still staring into the distance. "The flock is trapped . . . confused. It will be lost . . . unless. . . ." For the first time since they had been swimming together, he turned and looked directly at the Noble One.

"A very long time ago I witnessed a storm. It did not approach the magnitude of the storms to the north, but it was terrible nevertheless. I was but a Noble One at the time; the Great Drake who told me of the storm said, 'I now send you into that storm, because many will perish if I do not.'

"I now send you, Noble One, into a storm system with dangers far greater than any I faced; for if I do not, a flock will perish. You have heard the reports of the Snow Geese. Do not fly into the clouds, or you will be dashed to the ground. Do not approach the falling ice, for your flesh will be torn from your body." He paused to study the Noble One, then he touched him lightly with his good wing.

"Go, Noble One. Find the flock. Guide them to safety. Fly high. Fly swiftly. And do not look back!"

The Noble One was alone; the Great Drake had moved away. But it was not thoughts of loneliness that filled his mind as he climbed high into the air, nor even thoughts of the flock. It was the words of White Swan, who called to him as he left the water. "The strength

and wisdom of our Noble One will carry him swiftly
to the lost flock. With each passing hour we shall study
the skies for his safe return." She had spoken for the
Great Drake and not for herself alone, he knew, but
it was her voice that remained with him even as he
reached the cold, crisp air that lies far above the earth.

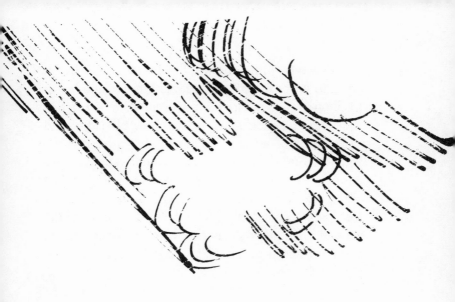

THE sun was high in the sky and the clouds had been building under him for nearly an hour. They were still far below, but he had been forced to climb ever higher in the face of the changing winds. Soon a thin layer of clouds began drifting directly beneath him. He could see through them to the layer below, but he had to struggle in the thinning atmosphere to remain airborne. Several times he dropped below the thin layer to search in all directions for any sign of the flock, and each time he had to struggle harder to get back on top. The lower layer had suddenly swept upward at a sharp angle and was protruding through the thin layer several hundred yards ahead of him.

I'll have to go up another five hundred feet if I'm going to get over that wall, he told himself, and began to climb in shallow circles. However, when he reached the desired altitude, he found that the wall had no end as far as he could see. There's no way around it, he groaned. But at least the winds are not violent at this altitude. He passed through a veil of mist that had already risen well above him. Then he gasped in horror. The clouds beneath him suddenly fell away like the vertical walls of a steep canyon only to rise again, perhaps three miles ahead, in a solid line of thunderstorms of such magnitude that their upper peaks seemed to look down on the sun itself. And even as he watched they were rolling and billowing to greater heights.

He began another series of shallow circles to assess the situation. For a moment he considered heading back in the direction from which he had come, but the wall behind him continued to build, and he knew he could never top it now. Lightning, too, was lacing back and forth along the entire wall.

"Nothing that flies could get over, or through that now," he whispered. "I'll just have to find another way out." He looked up and down the narrow trough. The dark floor was far below him and the walls to the north and south seemed to converge in the distance, both ahead and behind him. Descending cautiously, he found an altitude where he would have more control

over his flight performance. Although it became darker
as he descended, he could still see well enough to make
out the vertical walls. He permitted himself a few
moments to study them. They did not completely converge. An illusion of distance had probably led him to
think so at first. Bulges in the walls at varying altitudes
narrowed the passage. But fortunately, most were well
below him and he would not have to pass through their
restricted openings where the winds might exceed his
capabilities to overcome them.

After descending as far as he dared, he headed
northwest. The line of storms seemed to be moving
from west to east, but it was difficult to judge their
speed. The solid structure of the clouds to the south
did not appear to be as dark as those to the north, but
the frequency of lightning within them had increased
considerably. The northern line of clouds, however,
was not only darker, but pulsated with an internal
power source that changed from black to luminous
purple that brightened to a fiery orange, followed by
dull white, dark purple, and black again. He had seen
storms before, but nothing approaching these.

Cautiously, and trying to quell his mounting fear, he
descended a few hundred feet and began to search
right and left. There must be an opening somewhere,
he told himself. There has to be an opening. He knew
that if he could find one to the south he would soon
be in the clear, for he had just come from that direc-

tion. The same would probably be true to the north. Yet his search yielded no opening. Just as he was about to give up and search in the other direction, he saw what appeared to be a dip in the cloud tops to his right. It was not much of a dip, but a space of several miles where the clouds separated and formed a lower plateau. The plateau was still well above him, but it was an opening and he thought he could top it. As he struggled upward, however, his elation turned to panic.

I'm going through . . . can't climb any higher. I'm going through . . . can't turn back now. It *must* be clear on the other side! It must be! It. . . .

The gray mist closed about him like a thick blanket of fog, and he was becoming confused, uncertain of his direction. The thought that he might end up flying in ever-tightening circles honed the edge of his fear. He knew that he was losing altitude. He had climbed beyond his limits, and his wings would no longer support his weight in the thin air. He was going down and was beginning to feel the shock waves of thunder as it rolled through the skies. The throbbing light flooded his world with a living brilliance. The knowledge that he would soon be nothing more than a few feathers impaled on the stripped branches of a tree no longer mattered. The noise and the light were far worse than anything death could offer. He braced himself for the painful impact with the ground, and then . . . he was looking at a clear sky. He was free of the storm and no

longer falling. Instinct opened his wings; he did not
even remember folding them. He was still very high,
for he had fallen only a few thousand feet. The ground
below was wet and green and beautiful.

"I'm free! I'm free!" he shouted over and over,
unable to believe that he had survived such a terrifying
ordeal. But the ground was there beneath him like a
welcoming carpet, and the air around him was satu-
rated with sunlight.

Then the Noble One began to cry. He cried, not
from the joyous knowledge that he was safe, but from
a sudden, shocking realization: he, the Noble One, had
never once thought of the flock. From the moment he
had found himself wedged between the line of storms,
he had thought only of his own escape. The plight of
the flock had evaporated from his mind. They did not
exist.

"No, no," he cried. "I won't go back in there for
them. I'll be destroyed. I don't want to be a Noble
One. I just want to be free and out of the storm." But
even as he wept he was turning back. Already his eyes
were searching the clouds for another opening—an
opening lower than the plateau. The flock would never
top that. There had to be another way.

He banked, readying himself to climb the towering
wall, when something caught his eye. It was a pale area
in the billowing clouds that did not reflect sunlight.
Could this be a break in the wall? He raced toward it.

It *was* a break in the wall! Not the most promising one he had ever seen, but a break nevertheless. Whiffs of misty vapor floated about halfway up, an encouraging sign that there was little or no wind to drive him into the solid wall.

Now if it will only remain open for a couple of hours I'll get the flock through, he told himself. It's low enough in the wall so that even the weaker members should be able to make it. Such holes in storm clouds were not unusual, he knew, but their life span was highly questionable. Some would remain open for hours while others faded rapidly.

"I'll just have to hope," he muttered. As he flashed through the opening he shouted, "Don't go away, hole! Don't go away! I'll be back." Then as an afterthought he added, "And don't get any smaller, either!"

It seemed much darker in the trough now than it had earlier, but he knew that this was because of the sunshine outside.

"I'll fly easterly," he said aloud, trying to ignore the blinding flashes of light and pounding thunder that surrounded him on all sides. He knew that if the flock had made it this far west, they probably would have seen the hole and gone through—if they still had a leader. Many a flock, he recalled, had become lost and crashed to the ground because it lacked proper leadership. Indeed, without a leader they could easily have passed the hole and failed to recognize it as an avenue of escape.

First things first, he counseled himself. I'll search to the east, and if I fail to find them in a reasonable time I'll just consider another course of action.

He flew swiftly, studying every contour of the parallel walls, as well as the floor of the trough thousands of feet below, for any sign of contrasting movement that would signify life. Though he tried not to think of it, he knew it would soon be too dark to see clearly. Flashes of light were beginning to blind him, and he nearly missed the blur of motion that passed below him. "What?" he exclaimed, banking sharply. For a moment he thought he had only seen a spur of cloud poking up through the floor below. Then he saw it again. It was not the flock but rather a single mallard heading west.

What's he doing so low? he groaned. It seemed to him only reasonable to remain as high as possible without having to strain in the thin air. He had assumed that the flock and any of its members would know that this was their best hope for survival. He had forgotten for the moment their unpredictability. I'll learn as I grow older, he told himself. If I live to grow older.

The mallard nearly jumped out of his feathers when he looked to his left and saw the Noble One pulling into formation with him.

"Noble One! Noble One!" he screamed and squealed with such emotion that he would surely have fallen from the sky had not the Noble One struck him with his wing.

41

"The FLOCK! The FLOCK! Where is the FLOCK?" the Noble One demanded. "You can celebrate when we are out of this and still alive!"

The mallard, who was really very young, had considerable difficulty controlling his elation. He was all over the sky and would have fallen through the floor of the trough had the Noble One not flown directly under him.

"I ask again, Mallard," he said, speaking calmly, but with an edge to his words that was every bit as menacing as the thundering storms themselves, "where is the flock?"

"Back there . . . to the east," the young mallard managed, trying to catch his breath. "Lost our leader . . . fell . . . clouds . . . did not come out . . . nobody to lead us . . . finally got them to hold in circles . . . scouted to the west for an opening." He was talking so fast that the Noble One could not make out every word, but it was enough.

"Take me to them!" he ordered. "There is an opening to the west."

"Yes, yes, Noble One." He nodded excitedly and began climbing toward the east. "We shall survive!"

"Not if we don't hurry," the Noble One muttered. He was becoming increasingly concerned about the hole in the cloud wall. If it had disappeared he would be forced to lead the flock west and hope for another. They would have little time to find one. Moreover, it would be dark in the trough long before it was dark on the outside, and if they failed to get out before long he would not be able to control them. Many would simply blunder into the wall, blinded by flashes of light. Others would fold their wings and crash to the ground. But, one thing he did know for certain—while he was in control they would be fighting for survival, and doing it in an organized formation, not flying in circles of panic.

They had climbed several thousand feet when he saw the flock. They were massed in a pattern more oval than circular and drifting dangerously close to the north wall.

A couple more turns and they're in it, he thought with alarm. Without advising the young mallard, he began a fast climb on his own. At any moment they would spot him and come charging at him in wild jubilation. If he was to maintain control he must remain above them, at least for several minutes. He had just completed a one-hundred-eighty-degree turn, the young mallard close behind, and was heading west when the first cry went up.

"THE NOBLE ONE! THE NOBLE ONE! WE ARE SAVED!"

He did not immediately attempt to organize them, but rather continued his westward flight toward the hole. Finally, he called to the mallard. "There they are! Fall back and form them into V's."

The young mallard obeyed, and by the time they

reached the hole, which had, indeed, diminished alarmingly, they were in an organized formation. Less than an hour's light remained within the parallel walls.

"We must hurry," he warned the mallard. "The weather on the other side of the hole is clear and free of winds, but the passageway will soon disappear. I will go through first. You get the flock started after me. When they are proceeding in an orderly fashion, rejoin me and assume the lead. A few miles to the north you should find good feeding and rest."

The young mallard nodded and turned to the flock. "Follow the flight directly ahead of you," he called.

The Noble One dove slightly to pick up speed, and seconds later raced through the hole. Once outside, he flew on for half a mile and then turned to watch the first flocks emerge.

"Continue on!" he shouted to them. "The young mallard will soon join you. Follow him. He will lead you to feed and rest."

And the members of each flight called to him in turn as they passed, "Thank you, Noble One. Thank you."

More than a thousand had made it safely through the narrow passageway when the mallard appeared.

"Hasten to the lead," said the Noble One. "Get the flock settled for the night and then take them north in the morning. You are their leader now. Serve them well."

"And you, Noble One? Shall I see you again?"

"On the way to our summer lands," said the Noble One, "perhaps I can feed and rest among you for a time."

"The Noble One will be most welcome," the mallard answered, and his voice had taken on a new tone. The Noble One smiled to himself. The flock would be safe. They had found a new and competent leader. But even as the young mallard spoke, the number of flights passing through the wall was dwindling. Something had happened on the other side.

"They've stopped coming through!" the mallard cried.

"Go! Lead the flock!" the Noble One ordered. "I'll send the rest through to you. Look for them!" He turned and flashed through the hole. It was very narrow now and the once quiet winds within had become brisk and erratic. It took several precious moments for his eyes to adjust to the darkness, but when he sighted the remainder of the flock they were circling aimlessly again and would not enter the hole.

"Get through there!" he ordered, but none complied. As the Noble One's anger mounted, he felt he would gladly leave them to their certain fate. However, he suppressed the thought and asked calmly, "Why will you not pass through the opening?"

"We don't know what's on the other side," they answered. "We have seen many go through, but only you have returned—and you are the Noble One. Nothing can happen to you."

"Really?" he said in disbelief. "And what do you think is on the other side?"

"It has been whispered that Terrible Things might be there," they responded.

The Noble One could see that they were truly frightened. Strange, he mused, I can save myself and even lead the flock to safety, but how does one overpower a whisper?

"Come," he invited, "I shall lead the first four of you through and bring you back so that you may tell the rest what *is* on the other side."

The first four followed him without argument. But once through, it was only by threatening to toss each directly into the teeth of the storm that they agreed to return. When they did go back they wasted little time. "It's clear!" they called. "It's clear!" They offered no further evidence except, perhaps, in their fast exit back to freedom. The Noble One went after them, and for several minutes it seemed that all would follow. And yet, twice again he was forced to reenter the narrow opening and lead out small groups of the most fearful. Finally with only a few hundred remaining, he found himself for the sixth time in the trough. It was dark except for blinding flashes of light that seemed to sear his eyes. Somehow he managed to herd most of them together and literally push them through the hole to safety, while he remained behind. Only a few dozen were left when the hole completely closed. Blinded by the lightning and deafened by thunder, they cried out in dismay, "We're doomed! We're doomed!"

The Noble One did not stop to reason with them. He dove into them, struck them and shoved them with his powerful wings and bill, and then raced around to attack from another direction. They moved away in terror, and the Noble One permitted himself a short-lived sigh of relief, for they were heading in the right direction. The hole was gone, but the clouds might still be thin enough to penetrate.

"Go! Go!" he urged, shoving the hindmost group until they were overrunning the group ahead. Then they all disappeared into the wall, and he rushed in after them.

Powerful winds grasped him in a viselike grip and collapsed his wings with such violence that he cried out in agony. There was no up, no down. No rising or falling. Only spinning, rolling, tumbling, and terrible pressure on his body. Pellets of ice driven by the winds ripped into his feathers and gouged his flesh. For a brief moment the pressure slackened and he was able to move his wing just enough to protect his head. At least, he thought, the ice will not cut my eyes from their sockets. But the wind tore at his wings, forcing them open beyond their limits, and he cried out in even greater agony. He no longer cared if he lived or died or if the ice pellets did smash into his eyes. "The Noble One dies," he mumbled, as mind and body became part of the demonic violence.

Suddenly a golden glow bathed his eyelids, and he found himself staring into the sun. It was low on the horizon and yet he had to tilt his head back to see it. Then he realized he was upside down and the ground was not far below. Instinctively he rolled over and extended his wings, and the pain that ensued was greater than any he had ever known. A long, low cry was forced from his throat. The storm was still all about him and shock waves of thunder shook him cruelly, but he was outside the wall, a few hundred feet above the rolling clouds. Between waves of living pain he moved his wings in a series of gentle maneuvers to carry himself clear. But he was still falling fast.

I'm going to hit hard, he moaned. My right wing is damaged for sure. He tried gliding, spreading his tail feathers as much as he could. It helped some, but he was still descending too fast. A short distance ahead there was a small lake; perhaps he could reach it. The water would cushion his fall if he hit just right. But the ground rushed up to meet him, and the lake was still half a mile away.

I'll just have to walk it, he jested in his despair. That is, if some hungry predator doesn't find me first. Talking to himself seemed to help and he kept it up. Hope the ground is soft. Trying desperately to ignore the

pain, he forced his wings open a little further. The
storm must have stripped me of a few tail feathers, too;
I'm not as upright as I should be.

When he hit the ground it was hard, very hard. He
tumbled forward, skidded on his back, and came to a
stop against a thick cushion of high, damp grass.
Stunned, he remained motionless for several minutes.
Everything about him hurt, even his feathers. I'm alive
—I hurt too much to be dead, he told himself. The
question is how alive, and for how long?

THE Great Drake and White Swan watched the skies for the Noble One's return with the lost flock, but the skies were empty from the first yellow streak of dawn until the sun set in a red glow over the marshes. On the third day they saw a familiar form in the distance. It was the First Snow Goose coming back yet another scouting mission. Soon the Second Snow Goose came into view. This time they reported a clear passage north.

"We leave in the morning," the Great Drake said. "Tell the flight leaders to ready the flocks."

"But the Noble One . . . ?" said White Swan.

"He will find his way north with the lost flock, I'm

sure," said the Great Drake. "He would certainly not expect us to delay our departure on his account."

The next morning the Great Drake prepared himself with a good breakfast of his favorite roots and tubers. Then heading into the first steady breeze of the dawn, he began to accelerate for takeoff. Pushing himself with his one good foot while employing the other as a rudder, he tried to work up the necessary speed to support flight. The tip of his left wing served as an oar. Every few feet he would dip it into the water for directional control as well as added thrust. After a run of nearly a hundred feet, he flung himself into the air with a final lunge. Once airborne he seemed to hang scant inches above the water, his wings a blur of activity. Then with wings slowing, but now out of synchronization, he stretched for the sky with taut, elongated neck and a display of determination that left the watching flocks awed and breathless. "Such a feat could only be accomplished by a Great Drake," they marveled. "All others would have given up long ago."

The Great Drake gave a sigh of relief as he felt the air support his body. There were times in the past when takeoff was not always successful on the first attempt, but he seemed to have gotten the knack of it over the years. Yet the loss of many more feathers, he knew, would ground him for certain—unless White Swan carried him on her back. He looked over his wing. White Swan was already in formation with him.

She'd try to do it, too, he thought with a smile. The bond between the Great Drake and his mate was absolute and beyond the ornamentation of words.

He climbed slowly, as word was passed to all that he was airborne and heading north. The day was bright and clear, and soon the sky would be alive with the happy sound of countless flocks heading for their summer settlings. These were the moments he treasured most, White Swan above him and the Snow Geese off his right wing observing everything that moved. They would, he knew, give their lives to protect him and insure the survival of the flocks, and the thought saddened him. He hoped it would never come to that. Lately, however, the thought haunted him and filled his dreams. There was a darkness in his future—a shadow that somehow threatened the continued existence of the flocks. A time would come, he feared, when he would encounter difficulties beyond all endurance. But now his duty was clear.

The flocks are my concern, he scolded himself. Not dreams of some dark foreboding that are probably little more than a few days of bad weather, now that the storms have subsided. The sky is bright. The way is free. Just guide them around any lingering clouds to their northern lands. There among the many lakes and ponds they shall find feeding and rest, and those of breeding age shall raise strong, healthy young and prepare them for the strenuous flight south.

"And that had better be earlier than usual."

"What?" he cried out, for he had not spoken those words. He listened for them again, but there was naught save the wind and the beating of his wings. Yet he recognized the voice. He had heard it often enough before.

The voice had first intruded upon his mind shortly after he was elevated to Great Drake. It had told him of a lost white swan who had become separated from her parents during a violent thunderstorm. He had entered heavy black clouds and managed to lead her to safety, but when he had reentered in search of her missing parents, he was blown out the top. The young white swan had found him on the ground, injured and unable to regain his feet. She had nursed him back to health and never since had left his side.

Over the years the voice had alerted him to threatening storms, including the ones that had just subsided. That warning had come as no surprise, as the storms had been building for several weeks, and he had half-expected a summons. But when he was a short distance from the flocks he was on his way to lead, he had been startled to hear the voice again. "A Great Drake approaches," it had said. "He is known as the Challenger."

"A Great Drake, you say?" he had retorted. "Well, I shall test him fully to see if he has all the qualifications. Who shall succeed me will, of course, be up to the combined flocks after I'm gone, and I plan to be around for some time yet."

It was at that moment that the Snow Geese had spotted the Challenger. They had alerted their leader to his approach, unaware that he already knew.

Later the voice had told him of the Center of Attraction's foolish attempt to lead the flock. It also informed him that the Noble One had saved them and was recovering from his ordeal with the storm.

But now the voice's warning greatly disconcerted him. There could be only one meaning: To get the flocks to make an early departure for the south. This might well be beyond the capabilities of the Great Drake, he thought. It was one thing to restrain the flocks from flying north into the face of widely reported storms and quite another to move them from their summer settlings before they were ready. They would not believe that yet another wave of storms would come this year to threaten their survival.

Such are the responsibilities of being a Great Drake, he sighed. Always storms to worry about. But in many ways, he thought, Man was more to be feared than any storm or even the sudden freeze that gripped the feet of those caught asleep in shallow waters. Not only had Man tamed many of the animals of the land and the fowl of the air for his own purposes, but he was a cunning hunter, unmatched by any other species. He could imitate the calls of birds and conceal himself from their sharp eyes; and when he struck with arrow, snare, or gun he did so without warning and with deadly accuracy. Guns were the worst of Man's weapons. With a gun, Man could bring down game at very long range and cut a flock to pieces in moments. The Great Drake recognized the threat of Man's gun all too well. Because of the gun he had lost part of one foot and nearly his life and White Swan's as well.

The near-tragedy had occurred during a return flight after a long and pleasant summer in the north. The hour was late and the sun was poking long shafts of yellow through scattered clouds. The Great Drake was not leading, but was flying with White Swan behind the second V-formation in a long line of flocks. Apparently the first flock had decided to land, for he could hear their voices below. The leader of the flock ahead was already beginning to descend to the area from which the voices came. The Great Drake and White Swan followed, but when they neared the landing place, a lake of considerable size, he saw that something was wrong. There were very few birds on the water, other than those just landing, and they were drifting aimlessly, neither feeding nor making their usual noises. Then he heard another voice, one he recognized instantly. It came from within him and its single word of warning was clear and unmistakable: MAN!

"Stay aloft!" he shouted to White Swan. "I'm going to sweep over the flock and warn them to take to the air. Man is present!"

But White Swan followed him. She had never left his side, and she never would. The Great Drake did not have time to argue with her. Perhaps he would have given it more thought had he been able to see the faces of the hunters about to open fire on the flock. Suddenly, almost as one, they lowered their guns. They had spotted White Swan, and they marveled at her great size and the grace of her wings. Each waited for her to come closer that he might bring her down. Perhaps she would land behind that unusual creature she seemed to be protecting. He, too, would be an interesting specimen to add to the day's bag.

The Great Drake flew low over the flock and shouted his warning. "MAN! FLEE! TAKE TO THE AIR! FLEE THIS PLACE!"

"MAN!" The cry escaped from several hundred throats and even before it was fully out, the flocks were racing across the water and leaping into the air. The Great Drake began a zigzag pattern of short, sharp banks and turns to avoid colliding with them as they came at him from every direction. The guns exploded, and a mallard rising in front of him folded lifeless. The Great Drake was aware of White Swan's presence close behind him until a new burst of gunfire struck his right foot and wing and he began to fall.

FLY! commanded the voice from within. Somehow he managed to stop tumbling and maintain altitude, although his body was tilted twenty degrees to the right. He was also moving forward, more or less.

The guns were still firing but the pellets were falling short. As his strength failed, he began a slow spiral downward and hit the ground head-on. When he regained consciousness, the shooting had stopped, but he could hear the sound of excited searching in the distance. He struggled to his feet and immediately fell over. It was then he noticed that one side of his right foot was missing and that his right wing was limp and useless. Three times he made an attempt to stand and each time he tumbled to the right. He felt little pain; but that would come later.

The sound of Man was getting closer. Flying, he knew, was out of the question. Fortunately, he had fallen into some deep rushes, which were beginning to weave and sway in the early evening wind. It would be difficult for the hunters to detect any unusual activity within the erratically moving reeds; to find him they would have to stumble on him and, with any luck, that would take some time. Soon it would be dark; then he could easily evade them and look for White Swan. He felt certain she was somewhere close, waiting, not daring to move.

When night fell and the sounds of Man came no more, he called to her, softly at first, then louder, trying to make himself heard over the rising wind. He called again and again, and concern was reflected in his voice. "White Swan . . . White Swan . . ."

Still there was no answer, and a new fear gripped him. White Swan would make her whereabouts known to him if she could. Just as he was beginning to despair, a weak voice came from a dense growth of rushes many yards away.

"I am here."

Forgetting that he could not walk and could hardly even stand, the Great Drake half-crawled, half-hopped to the spot from which the voice came. What he saw made his racing heart nearly stop. White Swan was lying on her right side, her left side pierced by the shot. With great effort she lifted her slender white neck to whisper, "The Great Drake lives." Then slowly her head settled to the ground. The Great Drake moved close to her and spread his uninjured wing over her wounds. A light rain began to fall, and they fell asleep.

When the Great Drake awoke, the rain had stopped, the sky had cleared, and the stars were paling before the pastels of dawn. Although his body was stiff and sore, he managed to lift himself and move a little. White Swan still slept. He did not know how badly she was hurt. As he watched her anxiously, the inner voice returned, saying, *Go at once to the shallow waters and feed. The Great Drake must live. His life belongs to the flocks.*

But the Great Drake slowly shook his head. "No," he whispered, "the Great Drake does not leave this place until . . ." The voice now stilled, he arched his neck over his back and placed his head under his wing feathers. It was his place of retreat and solitude. After a few moments he glanced at White Swan, and his throat filled with a cry of joy. Her head was up and she was getting to her feet. He stumbled to her, ignoring his own wounds and forgetting, too (for the Great Drake was not totally unlike all others) that while his head was beneath his wing he had uttered a plea. It was not a prayer, for the Great Drake did not know how to pray, but a single word: "Please."

And the weather warmed and they went to the shallow waters to feed. Every day they gained in strength and their wounds continued to heal. The Great Drake learned to compensate for his injuries and soon he was flying again. Before many weeks had passed they were able to resume their journey. Along the way they were joined by two young, but very large snow geese. These snow geese had led the remainder of the flock south, and were now flying north again in search of the Great Drake.

"We were on the water when you warned of Man's presence," they explained. "Our leaders and many of our number were downed, but we were spared and were able to guide the flock south. We now wish to serve the Great Drake. There must always be a Great

Drake!" And from that time on, the Snow Geese were
the Great Drake's constant companions.

So intensely had the Great Drake relived this greatest adventure of his life, he had forgotten to check the condition of the territory over which he was flying. Now he looked down on dampened fields and flooded streams, reminders of the heavy storms that had swept the area in recent weeks. At least they had reduced the risk of an encounter with Man, he thought. Further north, the mountains and pine forests would offer protection, and in the Arctic tundra, few Men dwelled.

When, after many weeks, they reached the high mountains, the Great Drake kept their lofty peaks and ridges directly beneath him. Every day flocks would remain behind as each found their breeding grounds, and as they left they would call to him, "Thank you, Great Drake."

"Good summer to you," he would call in return.

In the land to the north that Man calls Canada, there are, nestled among the smiling mountains, sheltered lakes of such beauty that to look upon them is to know enchantment forever. It was here, among the snow-capped peaks, the towering pines, and the fields of scented wild flowers that the Great Drake spent his summers. This year, because of the storms, he would be late.

THE first few days of the Noble One's recovery were the most agonizing. Moving a few inches at a time, he began dragging himself toward the small lake he had seen in the distance, aware of cries for help all around him. About twenty members of the flock had also fallen into the field and were suffering from various injuries and shock. They had been among the final group to pass through the storm, and had been buffeted and mauled by wind and hail. Three were beyond help, having folded their wings and crashed to the ground even though they had penetrated the wall and were well clear. There was nothing he could do for them. For the others, it took three days of talk, threats, pushing, and even striking out with his good wing to get them organized and settled in relative safety on the lake.

Weeks passed and the summer was half gone before he had nursed them back to health. At the same time he had had to cope with his own injuries. Learning to fly again with a right wing that would not fully extend had been a most trying experience, but he had succeeded, and found himself as swift and strong as ever.

He stayed on until the last of the flock had departed. Each individual had thanked him, saying, "Please visit us should you pass our way. You shall always be welcome among us."

He recalled their words as he settled down to his last night on the lake. Although a Noble One is welcome to visit, he sighed, he is never invited to stay. He thought, then, of the Great Drake. It must be worse for him. The flocks seek him only when their survival is threatened. Oh, they make all manner of happy noises when he approaches and they certainly provide him with the best feeding places, but they never ask him to lead the smallest of flocks during periods of pleasured skies and untroubled days.

The morning after the rest of the flock had departed, as the first light rubbed the darkness from the eastern horizon, he took off. He did not know exactly where to look, but somewhere to the north beyond the chain of mountains he would surely find the Great Drake . . . and White Swan. He had tried not to think

about her. Yet, all during his recovery she had never
been out of his thoughts. He had dreamed that she
suddenly appeared and nursed him back to health, and
he had scolded himself the next day for having such
fantasies. Even now, as he flew north and called to the
flocks below, "Have you seen the Great Drake?" he
added silently, . . . and White Swan?

"Greetings, Noble One," they called back. "We
have not seen the Great Drake. He is far to the north."

Early one morning after a long night of flying, he
heard the haunting call of the loon.

"The Noble One comes! The Noble One comes!"

The loon's cry roused the birds still sleeping on the
misty lakes below. The Noble One called down a greeting and then addressed himself politely to the loon, for
the loon was a much respected bird himself and accus-
tomed to good manners.

"Good day to you, Loon. Have you seen the Great
Drake?"

"Indeed, I have, Noble One," replied the loon, with
a chivalrous sweep of his wings that brought him alongside the Noble One. "He passed this way many morn-
ings ago."

"Then perhaps you know where he has settled for
the summer?"

"That I do not know, but I have heard that it is not
a long flight north of here. If you care to breakfast with
me I shall inquire about."

"Your invitation is most welcome, respected Loon,

but I must hasten on while the sky is free of clouds."

"Please return this way again, Noble One. Word of your valor and leadership has already spread across the land. There is no fowl in the north who has not heard of the Noble One's abiding concern for all the flocks."

"Happy summer to you, respected Loon." And the Noble One hastened away to escape further conversation and flattery. Still, he was pleased that the loon had heard of his success, since this meant that the Great Drake and White Swan had also heard. For a few minutes he thought of White Swan and what she would say the next time they met. But the further north he traveled, the more he thought about the Great Drake, trying to anticipate his greeting. He would probably nod, obviously pleased, and say, "Well done, Noble One."

He was still deep in thought when he heard his name.

"Welcome, Noble One."

"Snow Geese!" he cried, "you are a most welcome sight."

"Word of your progress reached us many days ago," they told him. "You have traveled far. But now your journey is over, and you may rest and feed." They took the lead and said no more. For a moment the Noble One's heart sank.

"The Great Drake is well?" he ventured.

"Very well, and anxiously awaiting your arrival.

Each day for the past week he has sent us on an hour's flight to the south to look for you so that we might escort you to his summer settlings."

The Noble One's heart pounded with joy. He wanted to hear from the Snow Geese about everything that had happened since he had gone in search of the lost flock. But that would have to wait. He contented himself with thoughts of the Great Drake's company and the summer months ahead.

Soon they were descending toward a small blue lake. The Great Drake was off by himself, his head resting over his back. He was apparently unaware of the Noble One's approach, although the Noble One settled on the water less than twenty yards away from him. White Swan, however, swam up at once.

"The Noble One is most welcome," she greeted warmly. "We have long awaited your arrival." As she stopped close to him, the Noble One sighed. She was the most beautiful creature he had ever seen. How he longed to brush his neck against hers.

"The Great White Swan is most gracious," he heard himself saying in the polite mouthings of formal greeting he had learned were expected of any exchange between a member of a flock and a Noble One. Though it was not to his liking, he knew that the form of address was even more restrictive between the flocks and the Great Drake. He wondered if the Great Drake ever yearned, as he did, to speak without formality.

"Noble One, please feed and rest," White Swan said. She knew of his inner feelings, and longed to tell him that he, too, would one day share his life with another like herself. Even now, far to the south lived one more beautiful even than she, who was destined to mate with a Great Drake. But she only said, "You will find the feeding much to your liking. The Noble One must be hungry and tired. You will not be disturbed."

He was tempted to tell her that he wanted very much to be disturbed, that he would enjoy her company, but already White Swan was withdrawing. The Noble One realized that now, he too was within the protective buffer provided by the Great Drake's everalert companions, and that no one outside that buffer would approach him.

I suppose, he thought, I could simply swim away and feed with the small flock I observed along the south bank. No doubt they would maintain a polite distance from me, but at least they would offer a light-hearted conversation. He dismissed the thought. It was true, he was free to go; he was free to do as he pleased. But he would not . . . could not. He was the Noble One and he was sad and lonely.

He slept, but his dreams were troubled. He dreamed of leading the flock through storm clouds salted with wind-driven hail and blinding flashes of lightning. A muted voice from within spoke to him, and although

he could not hear it clearly, it drove him again and
again into the storm. Then, he awoke to another voice
—a voice he knew well.

"It is a new day, Noble One. You have slept the day
and night through. Come breakfast with me." The
Great Drake led the way to a protected area rich with
tender vegetation.

For some moments they breakfasted in silence.
Then the Great Drake spoke. "Tell me of your adventures since last we met. I have heard much of them
already. Word of your leadership was swift to reach my
ears. I am very pleased."

For several days they shared talk, fed together, and
at night slept side by side. The Noble One told the
Great Drake of the difficulties he had faced in the
storm, and of the times he had been forced to reenter
and guide the flock to safety. He also confessed his
terrible fear when he first cleared the storm, and his
reluctance to go back in. The Great Drake smiled to
himself. The Noble One would learn, as he had, to live
with fear and share it with no one.

The Great Drake asked many questions and then
began relating adventures of his own. He told of his
successes and failures, of the loneliness of leadership,
and the Noble One learned much.

"During a lifetime," said the Great Drake, "one
may encounter any number of adequate leaders. They
will, in general, perform well and accomplish the pur-

poses for which they were appointed. Great leaders, however, are extremely rare, appearing less frequently in a lifetime than the seasons of a year. Indeed, several lifetimes may pass before a Great Drake appears, is recognized by the flocks, and is unanimously acclaimed." He paused in deep thought. "Elevation to Great Drake is not something one seeks, or hopes for, or even earns by performing heroic deeds. Rather, it is an ordeal that befalls one because others recognize something within him that he may fail to recognize within himself." He paused for a second time and when he spoke again it was with difficulty.

"I have given of myself and it has not been a life I would ever wish upon another. Nevertheless, I must tell you now to prepare yourself, for one day soon, you shall be the Great Drake, with all its awesome responsibilities."

"NEVER!" The Noble One exploded with such vociferous conviction that even the animals paused in their activities to test the air with working nostrils and attentive ears. "I shall never be the Great Drake! *You* are the Great Drake! I know no other, nor shall I during my lifetime!"

The Great Drake smiled. How long ago it seemed that he had uttered those very same words. "Let us speak of it no more," he said. "We have other matters to contend with that may well test the wisdom and strength of our combined leadership."

The Noble One was more than happy with this turn in the conversation. He wanted only to serve the Great Drake, and he was pleased that his leader was now offering him that opportunity.

"Though the days of summer are still upon us," the Great Drake said, "I shall soon be sending the Snow Geese on an extended flight to the south. They will report on every condition of the land and sky. Storms, forest fires, availability of food and water, and the movements of Man and other predators will all be of importance in planning the southward migration." He paused again, as he frequently did, and the Noble One could see that the Great Drake was deeply troubled. Although the darkness of his dreams had recently taken on a lighter shade, they were now accompanied by a muffled, moaning sound that grew in volume with each passing day. He had been unable to interpret its exact meaning, but he knew that it represented some very real danger to the flocks—a danger that would be upon them all too soon.

"If we have advance knowledge of any unusual conditions lying to the south of us we can, of course, plan alternate routing," the Great Drake continued.

"Most certainly," the Noble One agreed.

"You, Noble One, will scout those areas to the northeast, the northwest, and the far north of the Great Islands, and report back to me at frequent intervals." The Great Drake was now speaking with the full authority of his position, and the Noble One listened attentively, nodding in understanding of the orders.

"Note the winds in particular. Have they increased in strength? How far south have the winds shifted at higher altitudes? Be especially alert for any unusual changes in pressure. And do not overlook the flocks. Where are they? How many? How long would it take to assemble them and bring them under my control?"

"I shall leave at once!" the Noble One cried.

"A moment longer," the Great Drake said. "Your mission will be more than fact-finding. I want you to meet the flocks and be known by them as the Very Noble One."

"The *Very* Noble One?"

"Yes, from now on so shall you be called." The Great Drake then summoned White Swan and the Snow Geese, who were resting nearby.

"We have a Very Noble One!" he announced. "Soon he will be flying north to meet with the flocks there and note any unusual conditions. We are so pleased."

"And we, too, are honored in the presence of the Very Noble One," White Swan said, bowing her head and unfolding her large, graceful wings until only the tips touched the water. The two Snow Geese also extended their wings and bobbed their heads joyously. "We are so pleased," they chorused, their faces reflecting the happiness they shared.

The Very Noble One, still stunned by this unexpected honor, nodded courteously to the Great Drake and then to White Swan and the Snow Geese. "I shall make my first report as quickly as possible," he said, looking once again at the Great Drake. Then he turned into the wind.

"Take care of yourself, my friend," the Great Drake called softly as the Very Noble One rose in the sky.

FOR the remainder of the summer the Very Noble
One was in the air from early morning until well after
sunset. Everywhere he went the flocks cheered him
enthusiastically, for word of his elevation had preceded
him. "The Very Noble One is welcome among us,"
their leaders would say. "Please settle and feed that we
may tell our children's grandchildren of this day." Toward evening he would accept their kind invitation
and gracefully submit to the prescribed ritual. When
all had paid their homage, he was permitted several
yards of uncrowded waters where he could feed and
gossip with them. After inquiring after their health
and listening to all manner of small talk and com-

plaints, he would settle down for the night, encircled by the leaders of the flock. Before going to sleep, however, he weighed all he had seen and learned during the day.

The Very Noble One reported to the Great Drake as frequently as his long flights permitted. On his most recent return he arrived just minutes behind the two Snow Geese. Visibly weary, but without complaint, they told of their findings.

"The land to the south, over which the terrible storms had raged, is now dry. The ground is parched and the grass stunted and brown. Many of the small streams and rivers are only beds of cracked earth. Even the great rivers are shallow. Where there is water Man has driven his cattle to its banks. Vast herds stand ankle deep in every available pool of muddied water, drinking thirstily. They are thin, their bones barely concealed beneath their hides. They have been long without water and food. Man, sitting astride his horse, seems to have fared little better."

"And the mountains?" the Great Drake asked.

"The streams and ponds of the mountains are low, but all contain water and will provide adequate feeding. The forests, however, are dry, and where there is water there is assembled every manner of predator—fox, wolf, mountain-cat, and even the hawk and eagle. All are nervous and fear fire."

"Thank you, Snow Geese," the Great Drake said.

His voice seemed strained and troubled. "Feed and
rest for the remainder of the day and night. Tomorrow
you must be in the air again. You will scout the same
area for any last-minute changes. On your return flight,
fly north along the mountains." The Snow Geese nodded and moved off to feed.

The Great Drake turned to the Very Noble One.
"Now tell me of your most recent trip," he said without formality of introduction or greeting.

"Uneventful," the Very Noble One replied. "The
skies are clear and remarkably stable, the atmosphere,
dry. It has not rained for many weeks. Water, however,
is of little concern because of the countless spring-fed
lakes. Indeed, the lakes reach out to the horizon in all
directions and each provides summer settlings for one
or more flocks. I spoke to many leaders and all report
that the pleasant days of summer are providing for all
their needs."

"And the air pressure and winds, were they normal?" There was a note of optimism in the Great
Drake's voice. Nothing he had heard yet suggested
major difficulties for the southward migration. Certainly it was dry to the south, fires threatened, and
Man would point his gun at every flock that came into
range. Undoubtedly many would fall to those guns and
to other enemies. All this was normal and to be expected—certainly not a threat to the survival of the
flocks. If difficulties were to materialize they would

have to come from the north, but so far the Very Noble One had reported little that would indicate such a possibility. Perhaps there was nothing to his dreams after all, and soon they would stop intruding on his sleep.

"Air pressure and winds were normal," the Very Noble One assured the Great Drake, "except to the far northwest where the two great land masses are divided by a narrow passageway of salty green water. There the winds have increased in strength, and I noticed a definite pressure drop."

"At what altitude did you observe the increase in wind strength?" asked the Great Drake sharply.

"Very high at first. But several days later when I again returned to check, the winds had dropped somewhat, and had moved farther south."

"This is worse than I feared," the Great Drake said, and once again looked deeply troubled. "You must go back at once! I must know more of these pressure drops and shifting winds. Feed and rest, but do not delay your departure by more than a few hours. I shall await your return." In a moment he had moved off and placed his head back over his wing.

The days and nights became one. The Very Noble One scouted and watched by day, and during the few hours each night he permitted himself to rest, he weighed and sifted the information he had gathered. Three times during those last days he reported to his leader. Twice there had been little change in the

weather conditions, and he had little to tell him, but
the third time a marked change had occurred, and the
Great Drake listened attentively.

"Thick clouds have formed over the waters far to
the northwest," the Very Noble One said. "I observed
them for two days and they did not appear to be
moving, although they expanded noticeably."

"The air pressure? Did it drop significantly from
what you observed on your last flight?"

"Yes, there is a very low pressure area throughout
the entire region, lower than any I have ever experienced. The strong winds have descended, too, and
branched out like the tributaries of a large river. If they
continue to descend, that stationary cloud front will
begin to move and . . ."

The Great Drake had heard enough. "The worst
comes," he mumbled, shaking his head sadly. He
turned to the Snow Geese. "Go now to the north and
northeast. Alert the flocks. Have them start south immediately." Then he turned to the Very Noble One.
"The Very Noble One will also depart immediately
and fly directly to the area of the high winds and
pressure drop. All the flocks south of that area must be
brought to me here without delay." He said no more,
but moved away slowly with White Swan close behind.

It quickly became apparent to the Snow Geese that
the flocks in the areas to the north and northeast were
not prepared to leave their summer settlings. "We

have no reason to think our survival may be threatened," their leaders argued. "The summer has been most rewarding and the fall days give promise of being warm and lasting."

"It is already well into fall," the Snow Geese reminded them. "Masses of cold air have been gathering strength in the northwest and soon the full fury of an early winter will descend upon you. Leave while there is yet time. Gather your flocks and assemble to the south where the Great Drake waits to guide you."

"Our eternal affection and respect to the Great Drake," they said, "but these weather conditions in the far northwest concern us little. The Great Drake need not worry himself about our flocks. We will guide them south well ahead of winter's heavy snow and frigid temperatures. The Great Drake may return south at his pleasure and rest assured that we will leave in time."

When the Snow Geese returned without the flocks, the Great Drake shook his head sadly. "They shall surely perish," he said. "They will not survive the winter that comes, for it will be the worst in more than a hundred years."

"We shall return to talk to them again," the Snow Geese offered without hesitation, although they had rested and fed only briefly. "We should have been more forceful."

"No," the Great Drake admonished, "you may not force them. But go; by the time you reach them they will be anxious to fly south with you. They will be faced with extreme difficulties and will lack the leadership to free themselves. Once you have assembled them, fly day and night and do not allow any to land. If some fall, do not go down for them though they plead and cry for your help. To do so is to destroy the flocks, for you shall not rise again."

"We shall do as you direct," the Snow Geese nodded.

"Do not bring the flocks here, for I shall be gone by then. Fly south until you cross the Great River-waters Man calls the Yellowstone. There, in the mountains south of its banks, I shall await you with all the flocks I have gathered along the way, including those now being led here from the far northwest by the Very Noble One."

"We go at once, Great Drake." Each in turn brushed a wing against his leader and nodded toward White Swan. In moments they were winging their way north.

The Very Noble One was bone-tired and hungry when he brought the flocks to the Great Drake. He had not rested for more than three days nor taken more than a few mouthfuls of nourishment. For two of those days he had worked constantly to keep the flocks in the air, and they had complained noisily. Every hour he had had to circle back and chase those who seemed about to descend. Now, settled on the Great Drake's summer lake, they could feed and rest, but only briefly. They had managed to escape the storm because it had paused in its surge southward. Why it had paused the Very Noble One did not know: perhaps to gather additional strength. But it would not be long before it began sweeping southward again.

All this the Very Noble One reported to the Great Drake. "The storm is not more than a few hours away —a day at the most. It approaches as a long frigid finger less than two hours flight in width but extending back as far as the eye can see. In two or three days it will blot out the land in all directions and nothing will escape its savagery."

"It is as I feared," the Great Drake moaned. "I have seen disaster coming for many weeks, but I did not know its extent and meaning until now, when it may be too late. I must try to save the flocks from the White Death, that they may not vanish from the face of the earth."

THE horizon to the north was totally obscured by the fast-spreading snow clouds when the Very Noble One sighted the vast assemblage of flocks. In desperation, the Great Drake had sent him out again only an hour after his return with the flocks from the far northwest. "Fly due north," he had ordered, "until you find the Snow Geese and the flocks they struggle to lead. They will respond to your leadership. With luck, we shall meet again south of the Great River-waters." Then he had turned away to organize the migration of those already with him.

The Very Noble One had hoped that the Snow Geese would be well on their way by the time he reached them, but they were still far to the north and were having little success in organizing the frightened flocks into controllable formations. Some huddled together on the ground, numb with fear; others flew about in circles, crying, "We're doomed! We're doomed! There is no escape from the winter that comes." Then they saw the Very Noble One, and immediately cried out with renewed hope. "The Very Noble One comes! We are saved!" Their cries rose above the howling winds. But the Very Noble One would have none of it.

"START SOUTH!" he ordered in a penetrating voice that clearly conveyed his anger. "OBEY MY ORDERS! OBEY MY ORDERS OR PERISH!" Never had they heard words like this. Certainly the Very Noble One was even more to be feared than the winter. It was even possible that he could smite them with a word if he so wished. Hastily they began to assemble.

"FLY SOUTH!" he ordered again. "FLY! FLY! FLY!"

Within minutes they were heading south as fast as their wings could work the air. "Do not look back! Do not pause! Fly!" His voice was less threatening now that they were moving.

Quickly he turned to the Snow Geese, who had joined him. "You take the lead," he said to the Snow Goose nearest him, "and guide them to the Great Drake where he waits in the mountains south of the Great River-waters." To the other Snow Goose he said, "Follow me," and dove for the ground.

The main strength of the storm had not yet reached them, but thick snow, driven by the wind, stung their eyes. "There are several large flocks still on the ground," he called to the Snow Goose, who was flying just off his right wing.

"It is true, Very Noble One," said the Snow Goose. "They stayed on the ground too long. Then the winds struck and the temperature dropped far below freezing; now their feet are held fast in the frozen waters. But the Great Drake warned us against going down to save those beyond help."

"Maybe it's not too late yet," the Very Noble One replied. "With any luck we may be able to free most of them without landing ourselves."

The Snow Goose did not reply. In the absence of the Great Drake he would follow the orders of the Very Noble One without question. In a moment they were flying only a few feet above the upraised heads of the hapless flocks.

"Very Noble One!" they screamed. "Save us!"

In their excitement they flapped their wings vigorously and stretched their necks upward as if to touch him.

Hundreds of them caught, the Very Noble One muttered, flying around them in wide circles. Apparently the ice has thickened so much that all the wing-flapping in the world won't free them. Then something caught his eye through the blowing snow—a herd of caribou. They moved slowly, heads down, plodding along in lines of four that disappeared into the distance behind the curtain of falling white.

"Follow me, and make noise," he called to the Snow Goose. "We're going to run a few caribou."

The Snow Goose nodded, and emitted such a loud, resounding honk that it startled even the Very Noble One.

"Wonderful," the Very Noble One cried, laughing with glee. "They'll never stop running!" It was the first time he had laughed in a long time, and it relieved the fatigue and tension that he had lived with for more days than he cared to remember.

The unsuspecting caribou nearly jumped out of their hides when terrible noises descended upon them from the veiled skies followed by unthinkable things with long necks and enormous wings bent on devouring them in their tracks. Again and again they were attacked, driven, and herded through the field of frozen water where the flocks were trapped. Here, too, they were greeted by ear-shattering sounds and menacing forms, and their heavy hooves moved faster, cracking the ice in their path.

"They're free!" the Snow Goose cried, his voice filled with admiration. "And only a few were trampled."

"So much for that," the Very Noble One nodded

with satisfaction. "Now to catch those who got off
first."

"Climb!" he ordered each group that he passed.
"Climb and do not stop until you see the sun!" As he
cleared the upper layer of clouds, he was relieved to
find the flocks holding to a loose formation. Quickly,
he organized them into smaller flights and headed
south. They flew the remainder of the day and all
through the night, climbing ever higher as the storm
spread before them in all directions.

"We must land," the flocks complained as the sun
rose on the second day. "We can't go on."

"You must go on or perish here!" the Very Noble
One snapped. "Soon we will find the Great Drake and
he will lead us to a safe resting place."

South they flew, often detouring far to the east or
west to circumnavigate escarpments of clouds that
none could top. As another day passed, many had
fallen and others were ready to fall. They had reached
the limits of their endurance, but neither the Very
Noble One nor the Snow Goose turned to look back
as they fell, pleading for help.

"We perish!" they cried. "Very Noble One . . .
Snow Goose . . . save us!"

"Fly!" the Very Noble One urged again and again
as more began to falter. "Fly!" And many found new
strength and flew on. Yet the Very Noble One knew
he couldn't keep them from falling forever. He, too,

was heavy with fatigue. He also suspected they had already passed the Great River-waters, but there was no way of knowing. Once he turned the lead over to the Snow Goose and dropped down for a look. But the winds and blinding snow forced him to climb back. He was near total exhaustion when he caught up with the flocks and realized that he, too, would perish if they did not land soon.

"When are we going to land?" the flocks began to chant wearily.

Fatigue and hunger and the unrelenting responsibility of leading the flocks under such hopeless conditions suddenly erupted in anger, and the Very Noble One passed back among them in a moment of fury. "You want to land? Go! You have my permission. I shall make no further attempts to stop you. Turn back! Let down into the wind. Fly as swiftly as you possibly can. When you see the ground—if you see it—increase your speed beyond any you have ever achieved before. And when you hit the ground you will still be moving backward faster than you have ever moved forward. Within the hour, hungry wolves will devour your flesh, even though some of you may yet have life in your battered bodies."

Again the flocks found renewed strength, but how much longer it would last the Very Noble One could only wonder. All had far exceeded their endurance and were more dead than alive. We must land soon, he

mumbled wearily to himself, and for the first time in
many days permitted himself to think about rest and how pleasant it would be to land. I could easily fold my wings and fall . . . fall . . . fall. . . . It would be so easy . . . fall and rest . . . rest and fall . . . sleep and fall . . . never to awake . . . fall . . . rest. . .

"Careful, Very Noble One!"

A voice intruded into his moment of peace. It was the Snow Goose. He had reached out with his left wing and touched him. "We have been descending for several minutes and are already skimming the top of the overcast. The flocks may panic."

"STUPID! Stupid! Stupid!" the Very Noble One railed at his own carelessness. "The wolves should tear at my flesh! I've nearly destroyed the flocks!"

He began a slow climb that soon had them well above the overcast. When he recovered his composure, he reached out with his wing and touched the Snow Goose tenderly—a touch of respect and affection that made further communication unnecessary.

"About an hour's flight ahead mountain peaks are poking their heads above the weather," the Snow Goose advised softly.

"I see them," the Very Noble One said, barely able to make out the dark shapes. He had always prided himself on his excellent vision, but he now knew that the Snow Goose's vision was much keener. "Let's hope the overcast thins enough for us to see the ground," he whispered to his companion. "When the flocks see those mountains we may have our greatest test in containing them."

"The ground has appeared," the Snow Goose announced a few minutes later.

"Then the weather is slowing. We have outflown the storm—for the moment. But landing conditions may yet be hazardous. We must control the flocks." That, he told himself, would be no simple matter. In their condition they would no longer respond to his commands once they sighted open ground. He had better think of something fast or he might lose them yet.

"Something moves toward us!" the Snow Goose cried suddenly. "It can't be . . . it must be . . ."

The Very Noble One strained hard, trying to distinguish between the mountain peaks and the dark forms that were closing in on them. Then his spirits soared; the millstone of responsibility lightened about his neck. There could be no question as to the identity of the approaching flight. The wings of the object below moved erratically, those of the object above, in perfect rhythm. It could only be the Great Drake and White Swan. When the flocks saw them, they came to life in an explosion of noisy cries.

"The Great Drake comes!"

"See! He is just ahead!"

"Admiration, respect, and love to our Great Drake."

They chanted and called again and again until the
Great Drake had joined them and was flying in formation with the Very Noble One and the Snow Goose.

Struggling to remain airborne, the Great Drake appeared worn and thin, and spoke without greeting.
"Twenty minutes to the south, just behind that wall
of mountains looming in the distance, are several miles
of open land not yet hidden beneath the snows. There
is ample room for all, but landing will be difficult, for
the winds blow wickedly, with treacherous indifference
to direction. Circle to the rear of the flocks and keep
them moving. I will space the flights and turn them
into the wind, if possible, just before they land. We
must hurry for it has already begun to snow."

"And what of the Second Snow Goose, whom I sent
ahead?" the Very Noble One asked.

"He has not arrived," answered the Great Drake.

"He'll join us," the Very Noble One said. "I know
he will."

The Great Drake did not respond.

By the time the flocks were organized into a work-
able landing pattern, the wind had increased in veloc-
ity as it came whipping off the mountains and swept
across the valleys. Many of the flights skidded when
they hit the ground, a few tumbling to a stop facing
backward. But all were quickly on their feet, and
within minutes were huddled together, asleep.

The Very Noble One was hardly on the ground

before he, too, was sound asleep. When he awoke it was dark and very cold and the wind was blowing near gale force, lowering the temperature even further. Quickly, he moved his feet. They had not yet become frozen in the shallow layer of ice-encrusted snow, but his body could not generate sufficient heat to prevent him from freezing to death if he remained there. What reserves of energy he had stored up had been consumed many days before.

In another few hours we will all perish if we do not escape this weather and find feeding, he told himself. He studied the sky, while ruffling his feathers to secure additional warmth. Dawn was about to break, and in the pale light he could make out the outlines of the mountains in the distance. He looked about for the Great Drake, but he was nowhere to be seen. Everywhere about him were sleeping flocks, huddled together for warmth. He was about to awaken them and alert them to the dangers of remaining motionless, when he saw White Swan approaching for a landing with the Great Drake in his customary place just beneath her. The wind gusted viciously as the Great Drake hit the ground, and he rolled and skidded for some distance before coming to rest. White Swan was at his side almost immediately, but the Great Drake was already struggling to his feet and issuing orders.

"We must have the flocks airborne within the hour. The White Death comes! Even now it increases in strength, and it is far worse than anything I have ever

witnessed or even imagined. Those caught on the
ground when it arrives shall never rise again." He
flexed his left wing slightly and winced as if hit with
sudden pain.

"You're injured!" the Very Noble One exclaimed.

White Swan nodded in confirmation, but the Great
Drake ignored their looks of concern. "There are
wolves, too," he continued, still trying to flex his injured wing. "Many wolves. More than I have ever seen
assembled in one place. Snow Goose is watching them,
but already they move this way. Alert the flocks!"

The Very Noble One did not wait for additional
information. He was in the air and racing low over the
sleeping flocks.

"FLY! FLY! FLY!" he called. "Into the air. Climb to
the south and FLY! FLY! FLY! Do not look back! The
Great Drake will join you. FLY! FLY! FLY!"

In seconds the air was alive with the flocks, and the
Great Drake passed among them offering words of
encouragement. How he managed to fly, let alone get
off the ground, the Very Noble One did not know. But
he was flying, slowly to be sure and with obvious pain,
but flying. Somehow he had organized the flocks into
formations of V's, and soon they were climbing.

"Some have not yet become airborne," the Great
Drake called to the Very Noble One. "They have been
encircled by packs of wolves and are now too frightened to flee."

As the Very Noble One watched in amazement, the

Great Drake swept in low over the wolves closest to the flock. There were scores of them, the Very Noble One judged as he, too, dove on them. The wolves sprang high in the air, and the Very Noble One just managed to escape their gaping jaws. White Swan and the Snow Goose joined in the attack from another direction, and together they kept the wolves in a state of confusion. But now another pack descended from the mountain to the north and began closing in; it was tightly formed and moved swiftly behind a leader. The Very Noble One scattered them with two dives, again escaping bared fangs as the wolves leapt up at him. He turned to look for the Great Drake, trying to see through the blinding snow. When he finally saw the Great Drake, he glimpsed him pulling up from a very low run. The Great Drake staggered momentarily a few feet above the ground, and then regained his aerial balance.

"Get these flocks into the air!" he ordered. "Get them into the air and lead them south! See that they survive! We shall keep the wolves away while you get them airborne. But hurry! Please hurry!" For the first time in the Very Noble One's memory, there was utter desperation in the Great Drake's voice.

"Not without you!" the Very Noble One cried. "I'll get them into the air, but I do not go south without my Great Drake!" As he began moving the flocks, he promised himself that once they were on their way he would return to the Great Drake to be sure he got off.

The flocks began to climb.

"The Great Drake will catch up with you," he called to them. "Keep heading south and FLY! FLY! FLY! Climb high that the winds may help you. FLY and do not look back!" He lost contact with them before they were a hundred feet in the air, but he knew they were climbing and heading south.

Now he would have to find the Great Drake in a hurry, for the ground was nearly blotted out. He flew very low in a search pattern that should have crossed the Great Drake's path a dozen times, but there was no sign of him. Several near misses with abruptly rising cliffs and wind-bent trees failed to alter the single purpose of his search.

"Great Drake! Great Drake!" he called again and again into the mouth of the howling winds. "Where are you? The flocks need you . . . I need you . . ." His head drooped low in utter despair and a sob formed in his throat. And then, in a momentary lull in the storm, a voice rose faintly. "The Very Noble One must join the flocks . . ." Further words were swept away by the winds, but the Very Noble One was flooded with joy. "The Great Drake lives!" he cried. "He is there!"

Ignoring the dangers of the wind and wolves—a large pack was not two hundred yards away—he dropped down hard and skidded to a stop against a crag of stone. Dazed, but unhurt, he shook his head and turned to see the Great Drake, and tears flowed from his eyes and he could not stop them. The Great Leader's left wing was folded back at an awkward angle, broken beyond hope of repair, and his stomach lay open and covered with frozen blood where a wolf had slashed him. A few feet away White Swan lay still, snow slowly covering her body. Yet, even in death she tried to protect her mate. One great wing was fully extended and formed a snow gate behind which the Great Drake lay dying, shielded from the icy blasts and thick accumulation of snow.

Injured when landing to warn the flocks and then slashed while diving at the wolves, the Great Drake lacked the strength to overcome the winds, and was hurled toward the protruding rocks just above. In one final and desperate effort to save her Great Drake, her love, White Swan had thrown herself between him and the rocks, her wings wrapped tightly about him. When they hit the rocks her breast had been crushed, her back broken. Her last words were for the Great Drake, and she whispered them with her final breath. "You must live, my mate, my beloved Great Drake. Your work is not yet finished. I wait for you . . . for . . . you . . ."

"Great White Swan is at rest," the Great Drake comforted softly, looking into the tear-laden eyes of the Very Noble One. "And so, too, are my beloved companions, the Snow Geese, one the victim of the storm, the other, of the wolves. They gave their lives

that the flocks might survive. Soon I, too, must go, for
the hungry wolves are but moments away. No, no, my
friend, do not weep. My work is done. Now you, my
Very Noble One, shall lead the flocks."

"I shall remain with you," the Very Noble One said,
and he wept deeply. "I will get you into the air. You
are my Great Drake. I will get you into the air."

"Go, Very Noble One, the flocks await you," said
the Great Drake. His breathing was becoming shallow
and rapid, his words difficult to hear. "You must go.
There is no other way." He paused, and the winds
howled. When he spoke again, the Very Noble One
had to place his head very close to hear the words of
his beloved leader. "When you arrive in the marshes
to the south, look about you. A white swan will greet
you. Though she is yet young, perhaps you will recognize in her something of the Great Drake, and of
Great White Swan who rests." His voice had grown
strong, but only for a moment. "Care for her," he
whispered. "If you love me, go . . . do not look back
. . . lead the flocks. . . ."

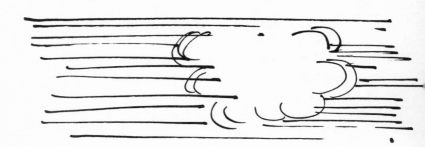

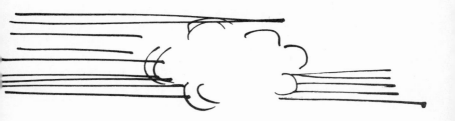

ND a voice reached his ears and though it was yet a long way off it spoke in tones of hushed excitement and expectation. "The Great Drake comes."

He was drawn closer to it and it became louder, filled with gladness.

"See! He is among us even now!"

And the cry went out, an announcement for all to hear. "The Great Drake has arrived! He has come to us. We are so pleased."

And he was filled with awe and wonder at what he saw. A living carpet of flocks stretched out beneath him, all standing high on their legs, necks outstretched and bobbing with unanimous acclaim, wings pumping in joyous accord, singing. And the voice he heard was the voice of the flocks.

"Welcome, Great Drake."

EPILOGUE

EPILOGUE

PERHAPS one day soon you may look to the skies and observe a great migration. Look carefully, for there, too, may be seen a Great Drake leading all the flocks.

Call to him, saying, "Welcome, Great Drake . . . Well done."

And he shall see you also and perhaps in time he shall return your greeting, saying, "Welcome, Man. . . . We are pleased that you are among us. . . ."